R.T. Taylor grew up in Hartlepool and joined the military as a driver. His adventurous attitude has led him to visit various countries around the world. Returning to his hometown of Hartlepool, he has worked as a professional driver for almost twenty years before taking up writing.

For Karen, my wonderful wife. For Rosalyn,
my loving mother.

R.T. Taylor

ANNA

To Judy

Best Wishes

[signature]

Carpe diem.

AUSTIN MACAULEY PUBLISHERS™

LONDON • CAMBRIDGE • NEW YORK • SHARJAH

A CIP catalogue record for this title is available from the British Library.

ISBN 9781788236447 (Paperback)
ISBN 9781785541025 (ePub e-book)

www.austinmacauley.com

First Published 2022
Austin Macauley Publishers Ltd®
1 Canada Square
Canary Wharf
London
E14 5AA

I would like to thank the following people:

Natalie
Lisa
Rachel

Chapter 1

A bright spring morning… and running late again. This past month hasn't been easy trying to get into a routine with a new, longer route to work, and sorting out the children out each morning is proving to be more difficult than she first thought.

Although Anna appears nervous, she uses it as her coping mechanism, but she has a secret inner strength that she doesn't mind using when the situation calls.

Looking up at three large buildings covered with glass, looking like Olympic podiums, each of them numbered and the bright red insurance company logo lit up on all of them. That's why they called it The Olympic Business Park. *I can't wait to see Rita and Lauren again,* she thinks.

In the lift, surrounded by mirrors, she quickly checks her brown, shoulder length ponytail and does the rest of her make-up. She applies a bit of red lipstick and mascara to keep up with Rita's flamboyant and Lauren's elegant style. Stepping out of the lift, she trots through the wide open-plan office to her screened-off desk she'd been given four weeks ago at her induction. "Morning, girls!" says Anna. "Even though I've been back a month, I'm so glad there are still a couple of friendly faces around here," Anna adds.

Lauren, one of her favourite work colleagues, is situated just behind her desk. Lauren, with her usual look of sophistication, slim build and switched-on, takes pride in her appearance; especially in her pixie cut hair. Lauren peers over the dividing screening, saying, "I've told Super you were in the toilet with lady troubles, not that you're a lady!" She throws a Tampax in a sealed packet onto Anna's desk with a wink.

"Bitch. But thanks," Anna says with a thankful smile. Rita, plump, curvy and tall, a larger-than-life redhead with a personality and dress-sense to match, glides across the office on her chair to Anna's space with a lollipop in her mouth.

"I can't believe we've been separated!" She shakes her wrist like she's thumbing a lift. "Just because they think I'm a bad influence," she says. "Oh my God, you know the gym they promised us?" Anna nods while sorting her things out.

"Well, it's only up and running, and apparently, it's for all three buildings to use."

"Where is it?" asks Anna.

"It's on the top floor of that building," Rita points at the smaller number two building. "The funny thing is, everyone can watch you exercising from the opposite floor of this building, but be careful... that's the same floor as the manager," she continues. The supervisor, known as Super to everyone, dressed in his normal smart jeans and wearing a super-hero t-shirt, creeps up behind Anna. "Nice of you to join us! Are you feeling any better?" he says in a quick witted but questioning manner. Pushing his Clark Kent style glasses further up the bridge of his nose, he runs his hand through his brown, side-parted hair.

With her back still to him, she says, "Yes, thanks," returning Lauren's wink.

"Can we all get back to work?" says Super, walking off in response to someone wanting his attention. All three roll their eyes and smile. Rita glides back to her work station, and Anna and Lauren settle down to work on their insurance claims paperwork.

Returning home after the school run, due to her lucky part-time hours, seven-year-old Luke and five-year-old Summer run in, full of energy. "Shall we go to the park?" Anna asks. The kids shout with a cheer, "Yeah!"

Watching the kids play on the swings, she notices Matt— her loving, supportive, rock of a husband of eleven years, walking over. With his gorgeous, brown hair as ruffled as ever, still dressed in his builder's merchant overalls, he walks over with his proud, manly strut. "Hi, Hun, how was your day?" Matt asks, smiling, wanting to know how work's going now that she has had time to settle in after five years off.

"Yeah, not bad, but I was running late. I have a funny story to tell you later involving a Tampax," she giggles. "But it's not the kids, it's the traffic. I tried to give myself enough time. It seemed to evaporate this morning. The girls covered for me, but the supervisor will start to check," Anna says with a little worried look on her face.

"It'll be okay," Matt says while putting his arm around her shoulders and giving her a little hug, kissing her on the side of her head.

Later, the kids tucked up in bed, Anna and Matt cuddled up on the couch, watching TV, and Anna lovingly turns and says, "Thanks for the reassurance earlier. I'm sure you're right."

"No problem, besides," Matt says, while giving Anna a quick poke in the ribs, "they know you could probably run that place blindfolded." He continues to tickle Anna. They fall onto the floor while trying to tickle each other. Losing their breath, they slowly calm down. They lovingly gaze into each other's eyes and passionately kiss. They make love there and then on the cream, deep pile front-room carpet.

The next day at work, having had another run in with Super, Rita glides over on her chair, dressed brightly and classy as ever, "Have you heard about the guy in the gym?"

"Ha ha, no…" giggles Anna.

"Apparently, he's in every day around 11am and he's fit with a capital F. We might have a wander up about 11:15 am to get a sneaky peek," Rita says with a smile.

"Ooh, sounds fun. We'll have to be careful Super or the manager doesn't catch us," says Anna.

Chapter 2

Two weeks later, Anna is sitting at her desk, typing away on her computer. Lauren pops her head over the divide screen. "Hey, are you looking forward to this fortnight-away, team-building trip they want us to go on?"

Anna replies, "What trip?"

"Apparently, there's more drinking alcohol than team building," says Lauren.

Just then, the supervisor comes over and Lauren disappears back down into her seat.

"Can I have a word, Anna?" asks Super in a matter-of-fact tone. Anna follows him to his office; they both sit down. "I'll get straight to the point, Anna. It's come to my attention that you've had a spate of late arrivals since you came back just over four weeks ago. I know it's nice that your colleagues have tried to cover for you, but management has noticed. I need to know: is everything okay?"

"Yes, everything is okay. It's just been a bit of a change around with the two children and the traffic; the new route to work. And I'm just getting to grips with everything, that's all," replies Anna, while looking out of the window trying to escape the situation and calm herself by meditating on the landscape of the town's rooftops.

"While you are here, you may have heard of the upcoming team-building trip. I can confirm that, yes, there is going to be one a fortnight away. Unfortunately, you won't be going as there are some people who still have more than a bit of work to catch up on and others need to get other matters sorted. I thought it best if you remained here and used the time to improve your timekeeping. Besides, there needs to be a trained first-aider around," Super says.

With a sigh of relief, Anna replies, "Yep, okay, thanks again for allowing me to return to my old position." Super nods with a little smile and Anna goes back to her work station, sits down on her blue swivel chair and takes a deep breath.

"You okay?" Lauren asks, popping her head over the partition.

Anna just nods and gets on with some work. Rita wanders over, "What's up, lovely?"

"Nothing", Anna says... shaking her head, "he was just letting me know about everyone's excursion and how I'm not going so I can work on my punctuality." Rita and Lauren both look at each other in shock. "Besides, there needs to be someone who is first-aid trained," she continues.

"Ha, likely excuse, you'll just have to try out the new facilities. Just think, you'll get to keep Fat Mark and Quiet Fiona, company," exclaims Rita, looking with an awkward glance to Lauren. Anna just rolls her eyes, gives a little smile and continues to work on her computer.

Chapter 3

A few weeks later, Anna is trying to get everything sorted, get the kids into the car and head off to the school then work. Arriving at her desk, she looks at her watch. 9:05 am. *I think I may be on time! And it's really quiet with most of the office staff gone,* she thinks.

Working away on her computer, she notices Super wandering over with a folder under his arm. He says to Anna, "Can you to take this folder up to the manager's office please?"

"Okay, sure," she quickly responds. "Can I run it up at break-time?" Super nods and gives a little grin. He walks away as someone calls him over.

Anna is in the lift with the folder to go to the manager's office. She realises she has never met the manager before, due to the company reshuffle. Stepping out of the lift, Anna glances out of the windows over to the gym, which is all in darkness. Arriving at the manager's door, she knocks, but there's no answer. Trying the handle and slowly opening the door, she surveys the room for the manager but no one's there. Anna quickly walks over to the desk, puts down the folder and leaves; closing the door. Heading back to the lift, she notices the lights are now on in the gym. It seems all but empty except for a guy running on a treadmill. She ponders about going to the gym in her lunch hours as there's nothing much else to do with her friends away on the trip.

The next day, Anna is working at her desk. Moving her legs to get comfortable, her legs nudge her bags. Looking down at the extra bag for the gym under her desk, she takes a breath, hoping for it be empty…

Heading for the gym, she has a few butterflies as it's been a long time since her last work out. Changed, water bottle and towel in hand, she heads for the machines. The door swings open and all the lights come on. She heads for a treadmill and starts some light jogging.

After a little while, the door opens and in walks the guy from yesterday. She doesn't flinch, and looks straight ahead at the mirrors and TV monitors showing the news and music videos, concentrating on her jog. In a bit of a rush, he jumps straight on another treadmill. Realising the time and feeling slightly intimidated, she stops the machine and heads back to the changing room. Passing the guy, she glances out of the corner of her eye and gives a little grin. Then all of a sudden, she lets out a massive, body-shaking sneeze. The guy immediately bursts out laughing, nearly falling off the treadmill.

Chapter 4

The next day, having really enjoyed the gym and despite the embarrassment, undeterred, she still wants to give it another go. So at lunchtime, she heads to the gym again and back on the treadmill. The same guy walks in again. He cracks a little grin and calmly gets onto the same machine as before. They're both jogging, looking straight ahead at the mirrors and monitors, not wanting to make eye contact, when he lets out a massive, body-shaking sneeze. He trips and his body slams down onto the treadmill, the belt promptly whipping him off the rear of the machine, and he lands in a heap.

Hitting the emergency stop, Anna quickly goes to his aid. "Are you okay?" Anna asks.

Slowly sitting up and clutching his shoulder, he responds, "Yeah, I think so." He continues with a giggle, "I seem to have hit my shoulder as I fell."

"Sneezes are dangerous." She giggles back. They both laugh.

After helping him up onto his feet, he says, "It's great to see someone else in here. I hope I didn't startle you yesterday? I was in a rush to catch up with myself after my meeting ran over!"

"Its fine," she says, looking down and sweeping hair over her ear.

"I'm Robin, and you are?" he says, introducing himself. Anna giggles. "Anna. Just Anna", she replies, trying to keep to herself. "Well, as long as you're okay, I'm going to have to get back to work," she adds. Anna hurries towards the changing room.

While sat back at her desk and trying to get some work done, she starts thinking about the moment in the gym. How strong and athletic he seemed, how confident he sounded and despite the sweat, how wonderful he smelt.

Chapter 5

Later back at home, having had tea, Anna asks Matt, "How was your day?"

"Ahh, you know same old rubbish. They couldn't run a raffle," he replies with a smirk on his face. "Oh, by the way, a few of us have been asked to go and work at another branch. There's a bonus on top of our usual wage for the trouble. Helen, the boss's daughter and assistant manager, has a reputation as a man-eater. She's onto her third marriage. She's said that she'll take the lads there and back each day, and if no-one says anything, she said we can claim fuel allowance too; and you know every little helps."

"Wow, yeah, great," she quickly answers. "When does it happen?" she replies.

"Next week all being well, we hope," says Matt.

The next day, sitting at her desk, she can't help but smile to herself. She arrived on time to work (heaven only knows how that happened) and things are happy at home. At lunchtime, she's staring at the screens on the wall of the gym using one of the exercise bikes. In walks Robin. He immediately looks at Anna and walks straight over to her and says, "I just want to say thank you for your help yesterday. I was really embarrassed when I fell. I'm sorry I didn't properly introduce myself yesterday, my name is Robin Williams, but everyone calls me Rob," and puts his hand out.

"I'm Anna." She blushes and giggles while they shake hands.

"It's okay, everyone finds it funny," Rob says to put her at ease. "I didn't realise how powerful a sneeze could be," he adds.

"Are you sure you're all right? It seemed a pretty hard fall?" she enquires.

"Hurt pride and a bit of bruising, nothing that time can't heal," he says with a smile.

He heads over to the treadmill, and gets on with this exercise routine. Anna notices him smiling at her. Embarrassed, she returns the smile.

As she leaves the gym, she looks over at Rob who is now on the rowing machine. She can't help but stare and bite her bottom lip at his toned muscles, and how he seems to glide effortlessly on it. Rob looks up, locks eyes momentarily and says with a smile, "Is everything okay?" Anna, realising she's been caught staring, gives a quick smile and hurries out of the door.

Sitting embarrassed at her desk, she starts to daydream about Rob on the rowing machine.

Chapter 6

At home, cuddling on the couch, Matt says, "It might be a really late finish tomorrow night, work have said they'll put us up in digs for the night so we can either finish late or the next morning. My mother said she'll pick the kids up and have them sleep over, so you don't need to worry."

"Yeah, that's okay." She smiles. She thinks to herself, *At least it's Friday tomorrow. I know I'll treat myself to the Jacuzzi. Mmm, nice and relaxing...*

On time at work and all caught up on her work, Anna is looking forward to her relaxing soak. Just then, Super wanders over. "Well done on everything this week, Anna. On time now and all caught up, good work. Keep it up," he says.

Turning around, she quickly responds, "Thanks!"

Feeling really good, she heads up to the Jacuzzi. Putting her swim suit on and her hair up, she sets the bubbles and temperature, and slowly slides in. Her eyes closed and her left arm resting on the side, feeling relaxed and listening to her favourite band, The Struts, through earphones, she can't help but feel good about everything. Rob walks in. He pauses at the doorway when he sees Anna just lying in the water relaxing. He walks over to the Jacuzzi, wearing only trunks and a towel resting over his shoulder. He puts the towel to one side; she doesn't hear or notice Rob getting in discreetly. Anna relaxes and sighs then accidentally slips under the water. Rob immediately jumps to her aid. Coughing and spluttering and wiping her hair from her face, she gets herself together. "Oh my God, are you okay?" asks Rob, concerned. Anna is utterly shocked by the situation of not only slipping under the water but also that someone is there. Rob lets go so Anna can catch her breath. "Are you okay?" Rob asks again.

Coughing, she swipes the wet hair from her face. "Yeah, I think so," she splutters.

"Sorry, I didn't mean to make you jump," he says with a little smile.

"No, it's fine, it's okay," she responds. "Anyway, I've been in to long so I'll have to go back to work."

"Okay, sure, but you don't have to leave 'cos I'm here," Rob says to reassure her. Anna quickly gets herself together and gets out of the Jacuzzi.

"No, it's fine," she adds. She heads for the door, wrapping her towel around her slim body as she walks. Rob is captivated by Anna's body as she walks across the room. As she opens the door, she turns to Rob. "Thank you, for your help," she says.

"Would you like to go for a drink?" he calmly asks. "Tonight," he adds.

Putting a couple of fingers over her mouth, she thinks for a moment, and realising she doesn't have any of the usual excuses, she says, "Yeah," with a little nod, thinking what harm can it do, as they are only friends.

"I'll meet you at that new bar, Hopes and dreams. About seven?" asks Rob.

"Okay," she answers. And with that, she leaves.

Chapter 7

At home, having had a quick shower, she throws on her favourite satin blue dress with lace detail. Still the best bargain she has ever bought from a charity shop, she thinks. A quick dab of her favourite deep red lipstick and a squirt of perfume, she's out the door. Rob is already at the bar with a pint hand. Anna walks in and makes her way over to Rob. He looks round and his eyes light up. His mouth opens slightly, betraying how beautiful he thinks she looks. Playing it calmly, he asks, "Would you like a drink?"

"Martini and lemonade, please," she responds clutching her bag.

"I wasn't sure if you'd turn up, some people are put off having drinks with their manager," he says. It suddenly dawns on Anna that Rob is the manager. Thinking on her feet, she responds, "Oh, that sort of stuff doesn't bother me." She shakes her head a little. "Besides, it's a rare night off," Anna replies. "My husband's away for the night and my kids are out too," she continues.

"Well, it's good to let your hair down from time to time," he says.

Anna gives a little smile. They continue chatting and the drinks keep flowing. The more they drink, the funnier the stories seem. They leave the bar and decide to go for a stroll down by the river; Anna links his arm for support. The moonlight bounces off the water and the stars fill the night sky. Anna feels like she's in a movie scene, slowly strolling along, and enjoying the moment and each other's company.

Anna suddenly slips and twists her ankle. She tumbles to the ground. "Ouch!" she shouts. Rob takes a look. As he put pressure on the area with his hand, Anna shouts again, "Ouch!"

"I think you've twisted it," Rob states. He quickly puts his jacket around Anna's shoulders. "You need to put some ice on that ASAP. I don't live too far; we can sort it out there," he explains.

"I can't do that. I need to get home, help me up," she asks. She is no sooner on her feet, when she shouts and falls again, "Ouch." Anna reluctantly says, "Okay, I'll go, but after I've had some ice, I'll go home, okay?"

"Okay, sure," Rob answers reassuringly. He helps her up and lifts her into his arms. Anna puts her arms around his neck for comfort. Stumbling into his apartment, he places Anna onto his throw-covered sofa. "Wait here, I'll go and get you some ice," says Rob. Anna looks around his modern, minimalist but stylish apartment. Feeling really tired, she leans over to her left to rest her head and has a snooze. Rob returns with a bag of ice wrapped in a towel. He switches on the radio for some relaxing music and sits down next to Anna. He gently lifts both her feet and places them across his lap and puts the ice in place. He leans his head back and rests it on the back of the sofa. Starting to relax, he begins to massage Anna's lower legs gently with his hands. Slowly working his hands along, passing the knees, he moves his right hand and places it on her tummy. Anna, still snoozing, responds, relaxes her legs and her legs move slightly apart. In her dreamy and drunken state, she forgets where she is and begins to imagine Matt is touching her. He continues to massage her leg and caress her inner thigh. Using his right hand, he begins to stroke her lace black knickers. Anna takes a slow, deep breath and after a moment or two, begins to slightly thrust her hip in an erotic way, then lets out a deep erotic sigh and lightly bites her bottom lip. He continues to gently rub her knickers and caress her groin. Anna, with her eyes closed, suddenly lunges forward, grabs Rob's shirt near the collar, kissing him passionately. He goes with the flow, slowly leaning over to his left. Swinging his legs round, slowly, he gets on top of Anna and they passionately embrace each other. Anna raises her knee up to his waist. Slowly and passionately they undress each other. Rob erotically thrusts his hips forward. Anna responds by rolling her head backwards and letting out a heavy breath and moan. Thrust after thrust after thrust. Anna writhes with passion and starts breathing heavily. They lock hands above their heads and Rob continues to thrust. Anna begins to moan and writhe. She screams with passion.

A few hours later and suddenly Anna opens her eyes; her pupils dilate with the realisation of where she is and what happened. Still naked, with only the throw covering them, she lifts herself up, putting her feet on the floor. Sitting on the edge of the sofa, she feels a sharp pain in her ankle. Sucking a little air through gritted teeth because of the pain, she puts her head in her hands, realising the gravity of the situation. With a bad head, in pain and feeling like crap, she tries to get dressed and leaves. Out on the street, she flags down a taxi. On the way home, she's filled with remorse, but she can't help but feel a deep sense of satisfaction. She has never had a man make her feel that way.

Chapter 8

Once home, she forces herself into the shower, puts her clothes in the washing machine and goes to bed.

Bang, bang, bang. Bing-bong goes the doorbell. With a jolt, Anna realises there's someone at the door. She scrambles to get dressed and remembers she must put on a brave face, even though she feels like crap and in pain. Opening the front door, the kids run past, throwing their coats wherever, and start playing with their toys. "Thanks for having them," says Anna with the best smile she can muster.

"Oh, it's no problem," Matt's mother, Sheila, responds. "We love having them, you know that!" she adds. "Mind you, you look like you have been up all night. Are you okay?" she asks.

"Just a late night watching a movie and a couple of glasses of wine," Anna replies.

"Well, you need to look after yourself, but everyone needs a little chill out time." She smiles. Anna responds with a grin.

"Anyway, I'm going to have to go. Father's waiting in the car; it's shopping day! And he doesn't like crowds," her mother-in-law says.

With that, they give each other a kiss goodbye and she leaves. At lunchtime, Matt arrives home. They kiss passionately and are interrupted by the kids latching onto their legs, looking for attention. They catch up over a cup of tea and then Anna tends to the kids. Matt makes a second cup of tea and goes out to the garden for some fresh air. While enjoying his brew, his suspicions are raised when he notices Anna's favourite blue dress hanging on the line. He decides not to say anything and tries not to jump to any conclusions.

Chapter 9

Monday morning, Anna arrives at her desk at 08:55 am. Rita struts past. "Shit the bed, did you?" Rita asks with her trademark giggle. Anna responds with her own little giggle. Lauren pops her head over the screen. "The trip was hilarious, you would have loved it!" she says. And with that, Rita glides over on her chair. "They ran out of Tequila and Sambuca." She giggles.

Lauren asks, "So what did you get up to then?"

"Oh, nothing really; sorted my time-keeping and caught up on my work," says Anna.

Rita and Lauren respond together, smiling and rolling their eyes, "Boring."

A few months pass and everything seems to be calming down at work, although she has never been back to the gym or Jacuzzi. There's a newfound tension at home but Anna is sure it'll pass. She sits at her desk, pondering over things. Rita glides over and asks, "Hey, Anna, are you looking forward to the Awards night?"

"Awards night?" says Anna.

Lauren pops her head up. "Yeah, we have an Awards night each year. There's usually a famous guest speaker," she explains.

"But the best bit is, it's a free bar all night!" Rita exclaims.

"Although it's not for a few weeks yet," she adds.

"We'll have to see what happens," says Anna, casting her mind back to recent events.

Gliding back to her station, Rita says, "We'll plan at lunch!" A sense of fear and dread comes over Anna by the thought of anyone finding out anything from the past few months, and she's hoping to keep a low profile.

Down in the canteen, the girls gather at a table to plan for the Awards night and eat a bit of lunch. "I've seen this amazing dress, a tad expensive at £150. But! Oh my God, it's gorgeous," Rita starts, trying to contain her excitement.

"Wow, really?" says Lauren with excitement. "I've found this classy number in my favourite boutique and it's in the sale," she adds. She pauses momentarily. "Only £95," she states, as if she's been savvy with money.

"You lucky bitch, always an eye out for a bargain you!" exclaims Rita. Lauren smiles and winks. They both look at Anna. "Well, have you found anything?" they both ask.

"Oh, I don't know. I'll find something," says Anna.

Chapter 10

At home, Anna is sorting tea for the kids. The kids ask, "When's daddy coming home?"

"He'll be home tomorrow; he has to work at the other store again," she explains. But Anna is glad of the break from the rows and stupid arguments over the chores, jobs that haven't been done or just snapping at each other.

A few weeks later, the girls are chatting over lunch. "Right, my outfit's all sorted, check, Lauren's outfit sorted," says Rita, putting ticks on the list. "Drinks, check." She adds another tick.

"Transport? What are we doing about transport?" Rita asks.

Laurens eyes light up, "What about a limousine?"

"Amazing idea!" says Rita. "Transport, check. Did you get an outfit sorted?" Rita asks Anna.

"I managed to find a lovely, red body-con dress with black lace chest and shoulders, black lace trim detail with black heels and accessories," Anna states. She laughs. "I found it all in a couple of charity shops on the high street."

"NO!" Rita and Lauren shout together, looking at each other in amazement.

With a jealous grin, Lauren looks away rolling her eyes and says, "I don't want to know how much." Anna smiles and shrugs her shoulders.

Rita bursts out, "Oh come on, you have to tell us!"

"£25!" exclaims Anna. "And the dress is Karen Millen and it's still brand new! It's still got the tags on," continues Anna.

Looking at each other in amazement, mouths open in disbelief. They both respond looking out the corner of their eyes in Anna's direction. "Bitch!"

"It's gonna be so great!" exclaims Rita excitedly.

After partying hard in the limo with plenty of champagne and lots of fun photos and having taken the long way around, they arrive at the venue. "Here we are, ladies, Richmond Hall!" declares Lauren. "I've never been to a stately home before! Let alone partied in one," says Anna. "It was the registry office and a social club for my wedding day!" She laughs.

"Well, this place isn't going to know what's hit it!" says Rita. "Charlie's Angels are here to party," she adds.

They make their way up some steps to the front entrance, looking like movie stars; their hair and outfits fluttering in the gentle breeze. Looking as glamorous as the location, they make their way in, walking through the grand oak doorway that looks as big as an ordinary house. They all gasp at the size of the huge hallway, with a sweeping staircase on each side leading up to the most beautiful and colourful stained glass window that looks like a simplified landscape painting. Above them is a large, ornate crystal chandelier. "Bloody hell, this place looks amazing," states Rita, heading towards the opened ornate doors revealing the grand hall. There are multiple magnificent chandeliers and stained-glass windows and large modern paintings on the walls. Anna says, "Should we find our seats?"

Lauren tries to contain her nerves and excitement.

"Yeah, then I need a drink," says Lauren.

"This place looks bloody amazing; 100% better than last time," says Rita.

As the girls head for their seats, the other guests can't help but stare open-mouthed. The girls giggle at each other, trying to take in the surroundings. "Oh my God, how breath-taking is this place?" says Anna in amazement. They look around at all the large artworks on the walls and the sparkling, large chandeliers, Anna can't help but smile. She can't hide how happy she felt. Super walks over to the table dressed in a stylish tuxedo. "Who are these three lovely ladies?" he says with a friendly wink.

"Thanks," they respond with smiles.

Chapter 11

Lots of food and wine later, the disco is in full flow. All three girls are strutting their stuff on the dance floor. Hot and a little drunk, Anna heads for one of the side doors and goes outside. She finds herself on a large patio area leading down a couple of steps to a very large fountain on full display. Anna walks down the ornate steps and makes her way around the fountain. Enjoying the light, cool spray, she stands watching it. She puts her hands on the low edge wall and sits against it, and enjoys the moment listening to the music in the background. "Hello again, Anna," says Rob. "You look radiant!" he adds.

She turns a little, surprised. Rob stands there looking pin sharp in his suit. "Thanks," she replies with a little grin.

"I haven't seen you in a while. How have you been?" he asks in a calm and confident manner.

"Okay," Anna responds with a little smile and a shrug of the shoulders.

"Have you been in the gym or Jacuzzi lately?" he asks. Anna shakes her head. Rob goes a little closer. Anna is hit with his sweet-smelling cologne and her heart starts pounding. Rob gently holds her hand, his thumb gently caresses the back of her hand and they momentarily gaze into each other's eyes. Drawing slowly closer to each other, the gravity of his lips is inescapable. Anna lunges forward landing a kiss on his lips. After a brief moment of kissing, Rob pulls back and uses both his arms to push her away at the shoulders. He really didn't want everyone at work seeing them together as people draw their own—usually wrong— conclusions and he can do without office drama. Rob tries to say, "I'm sorry, but..." Before he can say anymore, Anna holds her hand up to her lips and thinks how could she be so stupid—twice. Anna, realising the situation and with a shocked look on her face, hurries back to the party. Approaching the door, Anna composes herself by taking a deep breath. She no sooner gets back inside when Rita and Lauren come lurching out from the dance floor.

"We've been looking for you. We're going to the nightclub later. Are you coming too?" asks Lauren.

Anna, thinking it's the perfect chance to leave the awkward situation, shouts, "If we're going, let's go now! Come on, let's party!" Anna turns around and they make their way out of the doors.

Lauren asks them both how they're going to get into town as they arrived in the limo. Rita replies, "It's okay, we'll sort something out." Standing on the top of the steps, by chance, they see an executive minibus waiting. Rita nudges the other two and says with a wink, "Let's go down and sweet-talk the driver into giving us a lift to Hopes and Dreams."

The driver, unable to say no to three beautiful ladies, allows them to get a lift. On their way, they giggle and laugh at what happened at the party but Anna isn't as chatty, as the recent incident was rolling around in her mind, although she was still smiling to hide her emotions.

Arriving at Hopes and Dreams, they make their way in and head straight for the bar. Lauren declares, "This is my round. What's everybody having? Gin all 'round?" They all agree.

To which Rita responds, "As long as there's shots involved!" The shots are downed and they make their way to stand around a tall cocktail table; the drinks flow and flow! Shot after shot, gin after gin; the trio quickly gets drunk.

Then Anna realises the time and tries to say without slurring, "It's way past my bedtime. I have to go home." The girls beg her to stay as they think the night is only young. Anna sticks to her guns, makes her apologies and after hugging them both, leaves. She thinks to herself that if she goes home drunk, that will take the onus out of what happened earlier off her shoulders and Matt can tolerate her drunk. *He doesn't have to know I've been drowning my sorrows for blaming myself for kissing Rob,* Anna thinks to herself. Leaving Hopes and Dreams in the dark with the nightlife surrounding her, stumbling down the street intoxicated, she trips and stumbles to the ground, spilling the contents of her handbag all over the pavement. In her drunken state, she fumbles to collect her things. A strange man appears from seemingly nowhere and helps her up. She feels the strength in his arms.

Her left-hand lands on the stranger's chest to steady herself. Noticing the familiar smell—the same aftershave—it appears Rob has followed her. And once again, feeling the security of his grip, she lunges at him for a kiss.

A few hours later, Anna opens her eyes, slowly coming into focus and looks around the room to get her bearings. She soon realises she has woken up in a strange, dingy bedsit.

Quickly checking under the covers to find she is completely naked, Anna lets out a big, deflating sigh. She has the hangover from hell; she raises her hand onto her forehead to ease the pain with her cold fingers. Rubbing her eyes and realising she's in unfamiliar surroundings, she looks around for a clock. The alarm clock reads 3:40 am.

She turns her head to the right and as her eyes slowly come into focus, she realises she's face to face with a sleeping, complete stranger. Anna thinks, *Bloody hell, how can I be in this situation again?* She rolls her eyes. *I have no excuse. Why are these things happening to me? It must be that aftershave, it has a strange effect on me!*

Like déjà vu, she puts on her underwear and collects her clothes that are scattered around the bed, as quietly as possible. Anna makes her way out of the room and gets dressed on the way down onto the street, and flags down a taxi.

Sneaking into the house in the early hours, she makes a beeline for her bed. Matt doesn't move; always a heavy sleeper.

Chapter 12

The next morning, she comes down to see Matt dressed in his work trousers—a work T-shirt with a builders yard logo—and the children having breakfast. Anna makes herself a cup of tea and sits down at the table. At the same time, coincidently, Matt tells the children to go into the front room and play. The children ask their Mam, "Did you have a good time last time Mammy?"

To which, she replies, "Yes, thank you."

Matt reinforces the question the children asked, "Did you have a good time last night?" expecting a more detailed answer while having a drink of tea.

Anna, trying to put on a brave face, starts by saying, "It was really good! We arrived at this large, ornate mansion, Richmond Hall, I think it was called. It was absolutely huge; we could fit our house in the hallway, and the main hall itself looked like something out of a movie. And of course, the girls just had to get me drunk because it's been a long time since we've been out together."

Matt gets up in a huff and puts his breakfast things on the worktop, ready to be washed up.

"What time did you get in last night?" asks Matt.

"It was the early hours, I lost track of time," replies Anna.

"When I got up this morning, I noticed you had a bruise on your knee. Where did that come from? It looks nasty!" says Matt, concerned.

"I fell down the last step as we were leaving the stately house," says Anna

"Okay, well, make sure that you go easy on it, because you have two kids to look after all weekend as I gotta go in to work because they need more sorting out at the other branch," says Matt.

Chapter 13

Two weeks later, Matt is at work doing overtime again. Anna is sitting on her couch watching her children play, and out of the blue, she gets a call on her mobile. Looking at the mobile, she doesn't recognise the number but decides to answer anyway.

"Hello!" says Anna.

"Hello. Do you remember me? I helped you in the street a couple of weeks ago. You gave me your number when we got back to my place," says the voice.

"Oh… yes… how are you?" Anna responds in fake happy voice and thinks, "Oh my God I gave him my number!"

"I hope you don't mind me phoning, but I hope you had a great time. Would you like to do it again sometime?" the voice asks.

Anna tries to think quickly and says, "No, sorry. Can you please delete my number and never call again? Goodbye." Anna clutches the phone to her chest; her heart is pounding.

Having gotten over the weekend and back at work, Anna breaks off for lunch. About five minutes in, her phone rings again and it's the same mobile number as before.

"Hello," answers Anna.

"I'm sorry to phone you back, but I was worried about your knee and just wanted to make sure you were okay, and wanted to know if you'd reconsider going out with your good Samaritan," says the voice.

"Thank you for thinking of me in a kind way and the help that you gave," presuming they had sex, "but I've asked you not to call this number, I'm sorry to hurt you but I can't." Anna ends the call.

A week later, she gets a call from the 'good Samaritan' again and answers with, "I've asked you twice now not to call this number, I'm going to block it."

But before she has chance to, he shouts, "Wait!"

"What!" she replies, in a state of shock.

Calmly, he says, "I need to have a chat with you as you may have contracted something from me. That's why I have been trying to arrange a meet-up and I'm guessing at the sight of your wedding ring, you wouldn't want your husband to find out about what happened."

In that moment, Anna's heart skips a beat and her eyes open wide in horror.

After a few moments pause to collect her thoughts, Anna says to him, "Okay. Where and when?"

"Hopes and Dreams, 7 pm tonight, okay?"

Anna gets a cheeky favour from her parents to babysit as Matt is working late. Arriving at Hopes and Dreams, she walks in and heads straight for the bar. And because she's driving, she orders a coke. A stranger holding a pint of lager slides along the bar. "Hello, Anna," comes the voice of the stranger. Anna turns and there in front of her stands a tall, casually-dressed man, wearing jeans with a shirt hanging out over the top of them.

He introduces himself, "Hi, I'm James."

"Thanks for your help," she responds.

"Maybe we can meet up again sometime?" he suggests.

"No thanks!" she says, shaking her head with a look of disgust.

"Well, that's not what you were saying that night. You even gave me your number to prove it," states James.

"Well, I'm sorry for any false encouragement I may have given you. But I love my husband and I love my family. I'm not going to break up my happy home," she says, trying to be stern.

James leans in a little closer to Anna and says quietly, "Well, what would your husband say and do if he found out…" He pauses for a moment, "You have Chlamydia!" he declares.

"What?" she screams.

The barman and the other fellow drinkers look over in their direction.

She looks at the barman to get his attention. "Excuse me, can I get a large gin and tonic please? And hold the ice," Anna asks. She stares down at the bar; she can feel herself getting angry and upset. The barman puts the drink on the counter. James stands there, observing her reaction. She pays, puts her purse away and grabs the gin and tonic, and downs it in one. James quickly orders another gin and tonic. Anna pauses for a minute to try and get her head around the situation. Anna looks at James and says sternly, "Look, don't call me again and leave me alone!"

She goes to leave when James grabs her arm and says, "But you haven't finished your other drink."

She pauses, takes a deep breath then turns to look at James and yanks her arm free, and responds, "Stick it up your arse!"

And with that, she leaves the bar.

Dazed and with a sick-in-the-pit-of-her-stomach feeling, Anna walks along the street on autopilot back to her car. Thoughts rolling over and over, "How could I be so stupid? I've lost everything! How do I tell Matt? What about my kids? My family?"

Arriving at her car, she opens the door and gets into the driver's seat. Both hands perched on the steering wheel, she looks straight ahead with a depressed look and her eyes glaze over. Suddenly, covering her face with her palms, Anna starts to cry uncontrollably.

Over the next few days, Anna lives on autopilot. She does her best to put on a brave face with her kids and work. Although there is a noticeable tension at home as Anna tries to distance herself from Matt.

Friday morning, having dropped the kids off at school, Anna phones work to tell them she's running late and goes to the doctor's after managing to get a last-minute appointment. Feeling embarrassed, she blushes and asks the doctor, "Can you test me for any STIs please?"

The doctor replies, "Well, Mrs Mann, it's not the standard practice for doctors to do such tests any more, but on this occasion, I'll make an exception for you."

"Thank you," Anna replies.

"Although, I must say it'll take a couple of weeks to get the results, I'm afraid," the doctor adds.

Chapter 14

Friday night, the daily jobs all done and having put the kids to bed, Anna and Matt lay cuddling on the couch.

Feeling romantic, he starts to caress her breast over her jumper. Anna slides his hand away from the area. Seconds later, unfazed, he does it again. Anna slaps his hand. "Will you behave?" she snaps. Thinking she's joking, he leans forward and starts to kiss and nibble her neck. Slapping both hands down, one of them catching his leg, she jumps to her feet. "I've got a headache, I'm going to bed," she quickly snaps again and storms off to bed leaving Matt watching TV. Matt, thinking she must be stressed from work, lets her go to bed. The next day, waking up, Anna opens her eyes and turns her head to look at the time on the alarm clock which reads 10:25 am. *Oh my god, it's mid-morning,* she thinks. Out of bed and dressed, she makes her way downstairs. Half way down, she can't help but notice how quiet it seems. No voices, no TV sounds or people moving around. Anna goes into the kitchen to find Matt at the table enjoying a cup of tea.

"Morning, Sleepy!" he quips. Anna puts some water into the kettle and switches it on. Using her arms, she leans against the worktop and stares into space, and her thoughts start racing again. Matt, trying to be sympathetic, asks, "Is everything okay? Are you okay?" Her hand shaking, she pours the kettle in a clumsy way. Water splashes over the side catching her finger.

"Ouch!" she screams, slamming the kettle down into the worktop. Her mind in overload and with a huge feeling of being unable to cope, she starts to cry. As her cry becomes inconsolable, Matt jumps from his chair and puts his hands gently on her shoulders to help calm her down. "I'm sorry about last night," says Matt.

Her head in her hands and sobbing, Anna shakes her head.

"How could I be so bloody stupid?" she cries.

"What are you talking about?" asks Matt.

"I'm so sorry, I'm so sorry!" she cries.

"What's the matter? What's wrong?" asks Matt, worryingly.

"I've slept with someone else!" Anna declares.

"WHAT! You've done what?" shouts Matt. His hands slowly slide down Anna's back in shock.

"I'm so sorry," she says.

"What? How could you?" he shouts emotionally.

"I'm sorry," says Anna, turning around to face Matt but he storms away from her, back to the table.

"It's a good thing my parents came by to pick the kids up earlier! I don't believe it," says Matt through gritted teeth and shakes his head.

"I might have contracted Chlamydia," says Anna.

"WHAT? Do I have it?" he demands. Unable to speak, Anna shakes her head. "I need time to think. You'd better leave and move in with your parents while I try to figure things out," he adds while running his hands through his hair. With one hand covering her mouth and nose, Anna continues to cry. "You better not be here when I get back! I'm going to work," he states and walks out of the house, slamming the door behind him, making Anna jump.

Chapter 15

Feeling highly emotional and resentful, Anna goes upstairs, swills her face in the bathroom and packs a bag. Taking a deep breath, she zips up the bag, leaves and goes to her parents'. Waking up a few days later in her parents' spare room, she feels drained and depressed as Matt won't take any calls and won't let her see the kids. Forcing herself to get out of bed, she gets dressed and applies the usual make up, lipstick and mascara, as she must go to the shops. Heading out, walking along the street, she tries to reflect on all that has happened, she hopes the results from the doctor's come back soon and can't help but dwell on the mess everything seems to be.

After going to the few shops she needed to, walking along, she sees a sign for a coffee shop. She calls in and buys a latte then chooses to sit outside at a table that is shaded by a parasol as the weather seems warm enough. Anna, drinking her latte, ponders and watches the world go by.

Suddenly, she hears, "Anna?" The voice comes from a shadowy figure standing next to her table, blocking out the sun. Anna looks up to see James standing there. "How are you?" he asks softly. Her mouth drops open and she looks around in total disbelief at the sheer nerve of him to ask.

"How dare you? How do you think I am?" she says with disgust, as if it's entirely his fault. "After what you have given me!" she adds.

Chuckling, he leans over and states with a whisper, "What? Chlamydia? I wasn't serious. I made it up. I felt angry that you didn't care and it was the first thing that came into my head." Anna ponders momentarily, allowing the news to sink in and slowly realises that she didn't have to be in that situation. Anna starts to feel angry.

"I don't fucking believe this," she says angrily. She doesn't know whether to feel happy because she hasn't contracted it or devastated because of the huge mess she's in.

"Sorry, no hard feelings hey!" he says, not knowing the utter devastation he's caused.

Anna covers her mouth and bursts into tears. She quickly stands up, grabs her cup and throws what coffee was left at James. "Bastard!" she shrieks and storms off down the car-lined street, mentally dazed, clutching and fidgeting her handbag. Feeling angry and infuriated, Anna tries to mentally process the shocking and cruel secret James had just revealed. Different thoughts rolling over and over, she tries to comprehend everything. Anna crosses the road and walks through the nearby park. Mentally stressed, she starts to get a sickly feeling and her legs begin to feel weak. Anna makes her way over to a park bench and sits down. With the thoughts of everything rolling over in her head, she sits there, looking blankly at the ground. She opens her handbag, and pulls out a tissue and blows her nose, then reaches for a second tissue, folds it twice and dabs both eyes, cupping her face with her hands. With a thought of her kids and husband in happier times, she is overcome with emotion. She cries quietly and uncontrollably. Hearing footsteps approaching, she tries to calm herself down, not wanting to draw attention to herself. The footsteps get closer and then stop. She takes a few more deep breaths.

"Are you okay Anna? We heard you were sick!" come the two familiar voices of Rita and Lauren. Anna looks up while taking a deep breath. Realising her two friends are standing in front of her looking concerned, she starts crying again. Rita and Lauren sit down on either side of Anna and try to comfort her by putting their arms over Anna's shoulders.

Anna tries to explain, "I've made a complete mess of everything. Matt knows I've slept with someone else." Lauren and Rita look at each other, eyes wide and mouths open in shock and surprise.

"Bloody hell, Anna!" exclaims Lauren.

"Who with? When?" asks Rita.

"He was just some nobody," says Anna in a teary voice, not mentioning the manager to avoid any more complications. "I told him. I had to; because the creep told me I'd caught Chlamydia!" Anna states. "But I've just bumped into him and he's just said that he told me that to get revenge for not wanting to know him," Anna continues.

Rita and Lauren look at each other over Anna's head. "Shit," they say together.

"Well, you're a bit of a dark horse, aren't you?" Lauren states in a bit of tongue-in-cheek humour.

"You know what this calls for, don't you?" says Rita, winking at Lauren.

"G.N.O," Rita and Lauren both say together.

"What's G.N.O.?" asks Anna.

Rita answers in a light-hearted tone, "Girls' night out! It's what is needed in a situation like this. We go out and we'll let our hair down."

"Ha, you might but I've just had mine done. We've just come from the salon… remember?" Lauren interrupts, trying to be funny while shoulder nudging Anna. Rita rolls her eyes and lets out her trademark giggle.

Rita continues, "See, you'll find that going out and enjoying yourself with us will be the best medicine. In the morning, things will be different."

"No I can't, I feel and look like crap," says Anna.

"Ha, that's the perfect time. We'll look after you, don't worry," says Rita. "And I'm not taking no for an answer," she adds.

"We'll go to mine and get you sorted out. I'm sure I'll have something for you to wear," suggests Lauren.

With a forced half-smile, Anna mutters, "Well, okay, if I've got no choice."

Chapter 16

At Lauren's house—a two-up, two-down tastefully decorated terraced house—the girls sit on the front room floor with nibbles and glasses of wine in hand. Rita and Lauren are doing their best to cheer up Anna. "Hey, Rita, can you get us into that exclusive club on the edge of town?" Lauren asks Rita.

"Give me a minute to make a few calls," says Rita, leaving the room with her mobile in hand.

"Which exclusive club?" enquires Anna.

Lauren replies, "The Lounge! And talk about exclusive!"

"Don't we have to be members?" asks Anna.

"Not if you're Rita and you know the manager who is real sweet on you!" answers Lauren.

Just then, Rita comes back into the room and says, "All sorted, the Mercedes is booked for 7 pm and we have a table booked in The Lounge. Well, they didn't have any left in the bar area so we've been given VIP because he's so sweet."

"And he still is!" interrupts Lauren.

"Ha, it's like I say, 'take advantage of the world before it takes advantage of you'," Rita adds. Beep, beep. "That'll be the taxi," says Rita. They get into the taxi and go to the nightclub. Arriving at The Lounge exclusive club, the car turns into the driveway and pulls up outside the entrance where men in suits approach the car and open the doors. "Welcome to The Lounge," they say.

Inside the entrance, they're greeted by the manager, "Good evening, ladies," says the manager. "Rita, if you go to the VIP lounge, you'll be taken care of. Enjoy yourselves," he continues. Anna and Lauren smile at each other as the three of them make their way to the VIP area led by Rita. They walk past the bar and up some stairs. Everything looks beautiful and elegant. At the top, they come to a set of double doors with a man on either side dressed in tuxedos. Each grabbing a handle, they open the doors revealing an even more luxurious passageway.

As the ladies walk past the men, one of them whispers to Rita, "There's champagne waiting on your usual table." Making their way through, they pass local sporting heroes, celebs and business people. They find their table with three glasses of pink champagne and sit down; Anne can't help but feel good as her hands feel the soft leather on the chairs.

The girls, grabbing a glass each and wearing the biggest smiles, thrust their glasses into the air to toast the occasion with a chink, and shout, "Cheers." Lauren sits back, sipping her glass. "I could get used to this," she says. Rita and Anna giggle. As the night goes on, the champagne and cocktails flow. It's not long before they're giggling and laughing, telling each other stories and jokes.

The next morning, Anna wakes up in her parents' spare room. Feeling rough and with a banging headache, her hangover is softened by the thoughts of a fantastic night out. She thinks of how she hasn't laughed like that in a long time and that Rita was right; she did feel different. Forcing herself to get out of bed, standing up in only her knickers, she has a major dizzy spell and forcibly sits back down. "Shit, what was that?" she thinks. Trying again, she tries to get herself up on her feet but takes it a little slower. Slowly, she gets dressed and washed. Making her way downstairs, she's greeted with an empty house. Through the front room and into the kitchen, she looks for some painkillers for her headache. Having taken the pills, she makes herself a cup of tea and sits at the table. Gazing out of the kitchen window, she thinks about what she needs to do.

She mentally makes a list: I'll phone Matt about seeing the kids. *I must try and find somewhere to live too,* she thinks, *a flat perhaps. I'll try and get a sick note from the doctor, I'll say its stress, because heaven knows I am.* Anna phones Matt about Summer and Luke, and he agrees to her having some time with them. She contacts the doctor and manages to get a last-minute appointment, and gets ready to go to. Waiting in the waiting room, she can't help but get a little exited at the thought of seeing the kids at teatime, although she hopes that her headache is gone by then. Anne gets the call to go into the doctor's room. She walks along a corridor to find the doctor's surgery. Opening the door with a little knock, she says, "Morning, Doctor."

"Good morning. Come in, take a seat. What can I help you with today?" the doctor replies.

"Recently, I've had a lot of personal issues and I'm not able to concentrate on much because of the stress I feel I'm under—especially at work," says Anna

"Well, talking of personal issues, we've had your results back and they're all clear, which is good news for you," the doctor says.

Anna nods, "Yes, that's great."

"I'll give you a note for your stress, but first I'd like to examine you to make sure you're in good health. Is that okay?" the doctor says. "Is there anything else before I start?" he adds.

"Stronger painkillers for my headache," she quips. The doctor examines Anna; checking her ears, eyes, mouth and chest.

"I've given you three week's note, and, some stronger painkillers for your headache," he says as he tilts his head forward and peering over his glasses, "If it persists, please get back in touch," he adds. Teatime comes around and her headache is getting easier. Anna goes to see the kids. Knock, knock. Matt opens the door and Helen walks out looking all pretty, wearing a designer, red dress and a blue, short jacket. The light catches a gold locket embossed with scrolls and five diamonds in a row along one edge. She's talking to Matt regarding work. Anna has a shocked look on her face, Helen was the last person she expected to see there. "Hi Anna, How are you?" Helen says with a friendly smile.

"Yeah, yeah, I'm fine, thanks," replies Anna, stuttering with surprise, and puts on a brave smile. "That's a beautiful locket," Anna states.

"Thanks," Helen says putting her hand up to her chest to touch the locket. "Someone special gave it to me," she continues with a grin on her face as she thinks about them, "Well, got to go. All work and no play," says Helen and gets into her large four by four, and Anna walks in the house.

"Kids, go and get ready, Mum's going to take you out for a few hours," says Matt and the kids cheer, and go and pack their stuff. "How are you? You look a bit pale, are you feeling okay?" Matt asks in a concerned way.

"Yeah, I've just got a really bad headache all day and I can't seem to shift it," Anna responds. "What was Helen here for? Dressed to the nines," she adds.

Sliding his hands into his pockets, Matt explains, "I was going to tell you later but she was just on her way to a birthday party and she called in to ask me if I wanted the supervisor's job at the other branch because the one there at the moment is looking to retire."

"Wow, that's great," says Anna with an impressed look on her face. "And for what it's worth, I'm sorry for the hurt I've caused. The doctor's test came back negative, in case you wanted to know," she adds.

After visiting the park for a while, Anne takes the kids back to her parents' house and has tea as her parents are away on holiday. The kids go and play in the front room with some toys and children's TV playing in the background. Anna is cleaning up the kitchen when her mobile rings. "Hello." It's Matt asking her to have the kids overnight as he needs to work late.

Anna immediately agrees. "Yeah, sure. No problem. Thanks," she says jumping at the opportunity for some quality time with the kids.

Anna goes into the front room and tells the kids. "Hey, looks like you're staying the night here. How great is that?" she says in an upbeat and optimistic way. The kids turn and smile but return their attention to their toys. After watching a movie, Anna takes them upstairs to bed. All tucked up in bed, Anna reads them a story. Afterwards, she kisses each of them on the head; her eyes well up with emotion and regret. Turning off the light, she turns and says, "Goodnight, sleep tight, love you both." Life seems to be getting better and more positive.

Chapter 17

Having found and moved into a studio apartment, and returning to work, Anna hopes she can cope with the noise and stress of the office. She misses lunch because she feels nauseous, and a few work colleagues approach her to make sure she is okay as she looks so pale. This is repeated on an almost daily basis. A few days later, when everyone is returning back from lunch, Anna is sitting at her desk feeling dreadful and sick. Suddenly, she leaps from her chair, sending it rolling across the office between the other desks. She runs like crazy, one hand covering her mouth and using the other to move people out of the way. Slamming open the female toilet door, she runs straight into a cubicle, falling to her knees and is violently sick. Anna is sent home to rest. A few weeks later, things aren't improving with her headaches and she's getting concerned she's still suffering with them. Only now, with the odd, major dizzy spells and vomiting. Feeling she can't cope anymore, Anna starts to feel worried and contacts the doctors for help. Concerned about the symptoms, the doctor gives her a new sick note and sends Anna to the hospital's neurology department for a brain scan. After the scan, surrounded by nurses and doctors, she is shown to the consultant's office. Anne sits waiting for the consultant, looking round at all the models of brains and posters of the nervous system. "Sorry to keep you waiting," says the consultant sitting down in his chair. Anne sits nervously, fidgeting with her handbag. "We'll send you a letter to come back once we have your results. I know it may be easier said than done but try not to worry." says the consultant. With that, Anna leaves and walks back to her apartment feeling nervous and worried.

A few days of worry and pain later, Anna puts on a brave face for everyone, especially when she is with her kids. Having had lunch, she starts making a cup of tea when her mobile starts ringing. The screen of her mobile phone reads, 'no caller ID'. Reluctantly, she answers it, "Hello." It's the consultant from the hospital asking her to attend his office the next day. Anna has a look of fear and dread as she puts the mobile phone down thinking why have they phoned when she was told they'd write. Having made herself a cup of tea, she sits at the table, full of anxiety, and then tries to get on with her day.

That evening, curled up on the couch wearing her pyjamas and dressing gown, Anna tries watching a movie while enjoying a cup of tea. Her headaches seem to be getting worse each day. Anna starts to feel sick and starts to rub her stomach. With the severe pain and the feeling of nausea, Anna becomes emotional from the worry and stress for the appointment. Not knowing which way to turn or what to do, Anna acting out of desperation and feeling she has no choice, phones Matt. He answers the phone. "Hi Matt, I'm sorry to phone you out of the blue like this," says Anna sounding distressed and upset. "Because of my headaches, I was sent for a brain scan by the doctor. But today the consultant phoned me asking me to go and see him tomorrow. Would you please come with me, as I'm afraid of what the results may be?" Sounding genuine, Matt agrees as he still has feelings for her and she is the mother of his children. "Thank you." Anna sighs with relief. "See you tomorrow," she adds.

The next day, having picked up Anna, they arrive at the hospital, walking through the main entrance and along the corridor to the neurology department. Sitting in the waiting area, patients and staff are moving around and coming and going. Matt tries to help and reassure her. "It'll be okay," he says. Anna can only smile in response. After waiting patiently for a little while, the nurse calls "Anna Mann". Anna takes a deep breath and stands up. The nurse shows them to the consultant's office. "Please take a seat, the consultant will be with you shortly," says the nurse. They both no sooner sit down when the consultant comes in.

"I'm so sorry to keep you waiting," says the consultant. Anna clutches her handbag and fidgets with the strap. "Thanks for coming in but we thought it would be best to act quickly in these situations," the doctor adds. Anna, in a state of shock and disbelief, starts to go a little pale. Matt grabs her hand to help her cope, briefly remembering how wonderful it was to feel her hand again and gets a little lump in his throat. "We've looked very closely to your results and we have found a malignant brain tumour," says the consultant. The pair of them looks in a severe state of shock.

"I feel sick," says Anna, putting a hand over her mouth.

Matt, thinking positively, says, "Is there any treatments available? Chemo? Anything?"

The doctor replies, "Unfortunately, due to the type and size, there's nothing much we can do, I'm afraid."

"There must be something; we live in the 21st Century, don't we?" says Matt. Anna sits motionless staring into space, trying to comprehend the news.

"So what am I looking at exactly?" Anna enquires with a very shaky, emotional voice, with her eyes welling up and her bottom lip quivering. The doctor, resting his elbows on his desk, looks at both the computer screen and Anna's file.

"Well, if we prescribe you steroids and other medication, you may have six to eight months," says the doctor. "I'm sorry, I really am," says the doctor, sitting back in his chair.

Both in the car, they sit momentarily in silence in shock, when Anna breaks down crying. Matt can't help but get overwhelmed too and puts his arms across her shoulders and gently pulls Anna towards him, and they hug. Holding each other tightly, they cry in each other's arms, both enjoying each other's affections. Calming down and wiping her tears, Anna asks Matt emotionally, "Can you take me home please?" Anna takes out a tissue from her bag and wipes the tears from her cheek and eyes, and gently blows her nose.

"Yes, no problem. I'm sorry I have to go back to work," says Matt, realising the harsh reality of splitting up, "Will you be okay?" he adds.

"I don't know!" replies Anna, taking deep breaths to try and calm down. "I'm going to go round and break the news to my parents," she adds, wiping more tears away. Arriving at her apartment, Anne slowly opens the car door. "Thanks for going with me and for your support," she says in a soft tone. "No problem. Will you be okay?" Matt asks.

Anna responds while putting on a brave face, "Yeah, I'll be okay." Matt watches Anna go in and pauses for a moment to collect his thoughts, and sets off back to work. Later that day, Matt and the kids have just finished tea. Matt is sitting on the sofa in the house, thinking of the devastating news Anna has just received.

He takes his kids and goes to his parents, and explains everything that's happened and comes up with an idea. He asks them to look after Summer and Luke because he needs to sort things out with Anna. Matt arrives at Anna's place and knocks on the door. The door opens slowly and a pair of red, tired eyes appears in the gap. "Anna, can I come in, please? I want to discuss something with you," asks Matt. Anna, dressed in pyjamas and dressing gown, swings the door open and turns to go inside.

"Yeah, come in," she says in a tired voice.

Following her in, Anna sits down, and Matt stays standing and says, "Despite everything that's happened, I can't bear to see you like this, and given the news, I think it would be for the best for everyone if you were to move back home. That way, the kids will get…" Anna jumps up and tightly hugs Matt.

"Thank you," says Anna emotionally.

Over the next few days, Anna finally starts to get some pain relief thanks to the new medication the hospital has put her on even if they come with a few side effects like anger, depression and feeling upset. She quickly settles in back at home even if she and Matt aren't back together, he's happy to do the right thing for her and the children, but is still reeling from the hurt. At least she'll be around the children and Matt has agreed to helping out with anything. Anna arranges to go to her workplace to give her notice and on arrival, is greeted by Lauren and Rita who are emotional wrecks and a few other colleagues. After a lot of hugs and goodbyes, Super appears from his office. "We were just starting to like you," says Super, trying to lighten the mood. Anna walks up to Super and gives him a hug. "Thanks for everything," Anna says emotionally into his ear and kisses him on the cheek. Anna steps back: Super tries to compose himself by straightening his top and wiping a tear from his eye. Lauren approaches Super and puts her hand on his arm for support, thinking he's a big softy really.

Clearing his throat to get rid of his emotional lump, he says, "We've all had a whip round from all three buildings to help you in the future, we wish you all the best. If there's anything we or the company can do to help, please let us know." Handing over a card and envelope with a substantial amount of cash inside.

After having final hugs and thanking everyone for everything, Anna leaves and makes her way back to the car. Once outside, she pulls out the envelope and looks inside at all the notes. Flicking her thumb across the notes, Anna has an idea and heads off into town. Arriving at her bank, Anna walks in and approaches the counter. "Hi, I want to deposit this money into my children's accounts. I don't have their bank books but I have my bank card. Would you be able to help?" asks Anna with a hopeful look on her face.

The bank clerk pauses for a moment but with a smile, the clerk nods her head and says, "Sure, no problem." Relieved by the thought of helping her kids, Anna heads back to her car. Walking past all the shops, Anna starts to notice all the little things going on around her: the young children pestering their parents for sweets; the young ladies enjoying coffees in the café and the couples walking along, holding hands. Arriving and getting into the car, Anna feels really angry.

Letting out a big scream and hitting the steering wheel with the palm of her hand, she thinks how life isn't fair; she may have done some wrong things but she doesn't deserve this. Getting a tissue out of her handbag, she wipes the tears away from the inner corners of her eyes. Calming down slightly, she starts the engine and makes her way home. Driving down the street, she listens to her favourite band, The Struts, really loud to try and calm down. Enjoying the loud music and dancing so much, she drives through a red light. She decides to take the long route home so the euphoric feeling lasts as long as possible; only listening to her favourite band helps her get lost in the moment.

Chapter 18

Arriving home, she notices Matt's car parked up. Anna goes in to find Matt sitting in the kitchen, enjoying a cup of tea. "You're home early, is everything okay?" asks Anna.

"A bit of a good news! They've given me time to be at home. Basically, they'll phone me each night to let me know if I'm needed at work and let me come home when I'm not needed to help with everything," says Matt.

"Wow, that's great," Anna responds. Matt walks over to Anna and gives her a hug.

A few days go by and things seem to be settling down again. Laughter and fun is filling the air each day. Spending time with the kids and each other, and Matt only getting called into work on an ad-hoc basis is really helping the family to unite. Anna starts to think generally about funeral plans whenever she has a few minutes to herself. So one morning, after doing a lot of thinking, she decides to ask Matt to contribute. Not the subject they were expecting to have, but Matt agrees to help and put any plans into place. To lighten the mood, Matt has an idea. "Hey, now that we have gotten that out of the way, what would you say to a day at the seaside tomorrow, just us?" he asks.

"That sounds like a great idea," Anna says, smiling, jumping at the opportunity. "I can't wait," she adds.

The next day, Anna and Matt get the children ready for school and drop them off. Waving goodbye as they disappear among the other children, Anna turns and looks at Matt and smiles. "Are you ready to go to the seaside?" asks Matt. Anna smiles, and nods with excitement and anticipation.

After driving for a while, they arrive at the seaside. Getting out of the car, Anna's hair moves gently in the wind. She puts her face towards the sun to feel the warm glow and takes a deep breath. "Ah, smell that lovely sea air." Matt smiles back. Armed only with their coats, they make their way to the promenade and walk along towards the long wooden pier with amusements and seaside novelty shops on it. Walking along, Matt with his hands in his jean pockets and Anna next to him with her arm interlocked with his, they come across a vintage style ice cream van. "Let's get one!" suggests Matt.

Anna smiles and nods. "Yes, please," she replies. Ice creams in hand, they continue along the promenade. "Stop a minute, I want to take a picture," says Anna. Standing close to each other, holding their ice creams up and pulling funny faces and sticking their tongues out. Both of them look at the picture and laugh then continue their stroll. Lick after lick, they enjoy the ice creams, come to the wooden pier and make their way along it. The smell of fish and chips fills the air, and the sound of seagulls and waves crashing echo around them. Anna's hair flutters in the increased wind. "What a beautiful day," states Anna. Meanwhile, Matt spots some seaside oddity on the style of cartoon characters painted on a large piece of board with the heads missing and a notch for people to put their chins, while finishing their ice creams.

"Come on, we'll get someone to take a picture!" says Matt. Again, they stand together laughing at the picture. Anna holding onto the rail of the pier, they walk further along. They come to a fish and chip shop, "Fancy sharing some chips?" asks Matt.

"Only if you put salt and vinegar on them," replies Anna with a smile. They sit on a wooden bench nearby, Matt holding the chips in hand, and because they're so hot, they use wooden forks to stab the chips. Sharing the chips, savouring the sunshine and the gentle breeze, they enjoy the view, looking out across the sea to the cliffs in the distance that marks the end of the beach. The fishing boats bob along the wavy water and the seagulls fly around. Finishing their chips and putting the paper in the bin, they walk over to the pier railings and lean on them. They both look out at the picture-perfect postcard scene, they look at each other and smile. "Thank you for today, it's been really special for me," says Anna. Tears forming in her eyes, she gives him a quick kiss on his lips. Matt looks into her eyes again and slowly leans in to kiss her. As their lips touch, they begin to slowly kiss passionately. Holding each other tightly and kissing with such passion, anyone could mistake them for the perfect couple.

Back in the car on the way home, Anna falls asleep, exhausted from the day's events and the medication she is on. Back in town, they go and collect the children from school, and go home. Enjoying a cup of tea, they reminisce over the day's activities, looking and smiling at each other like the used to do.

Chapter 19

Over the next few days, Anna feels like recent history has been wiped away. Waking up, the bright sunshine shines directly into the bedroom. Anna gets up, dresses and goes downstairs. Matt is sitting at the table enjoying a cup of tea, having gotten the children off to school. "How do you feel about looking after me when I'm really sick? I mean I don't want to be a burden on you or anyone," Anna asks. Matt stares into space, unsure how to answer.

"Well, we'll just have to cross each bridge when we get to it. Whatever happens, happens! We'll deal with it then," answers Matt sympathetically. "I'm really sorry but I've got to go into work this morning. Hopefully I'll be back home after lunch," he adds.

"Okay," responds Anna with a smile. With that, Matt quickly kisses her on the top of the head and leaves for work.

Mid-afternoon, Matt unlocks the door. Walking in, he shouts, "Hi Honey, I'm home." a still silence is in the air. Matt, presuming Anna has popped out, makes his way upstairs to get changed. Walking into the bedroom, he sees the outline of Anna's body under the covers with her back to him. Walking around the bed, Matt says in a playful way, "Wake up, Sleepy head. I'm home." Sitting down beside her, she hasn't moved and her eyes are still closed. Matt, using the back of his fingers, strokes her face gently. Anna is ice cold to the touch and Matt notices stillness to her eyelids. Looking over to the bedside cabinet, the bottles of pills are all empty and the slow realisation dawns on Matt. He quickly checks her pulse—nothing. Anna is dead. Matt's bottom lip starts to quiver. He starts to brush her hair with his hand and tears start to roll down his face. Knowing she was out of pain and finally at peace give Matt little comfort as the tears keep streaming. *Giving someone the burden of looking after her was obviously too much for her,* Matt thinks.

Everyone is dressed in black. Family and friends gather around the coffin covered in flowers and wreaths. The priest says a prayer and a few choice notes. Matt comforts an upset Summer and Luke, standing in front of both his and Anna's parents. Rita, Lauren and Super look on from the middle of the guests. The coffin goes into the ground. "Ashes to ashes, dust to dust," says the priest. A selected few guests throw small handfuls of dirt onto the coffin and say their goodbyes. Each one files past Matt and the children to pass on their condolences in their time of grief.

Laid in bed, sprawled diagonally in the double bed, Matt's eyes begin to flutter awake to the sound of distant voices. His eyes look around the room, while he tries to figure out what the sounds are. The voices sound familiar but he can't figure out who or what's going on. Thinking it might be the neighbours having a domestic or party, he turns his head around and squints his eyes to read the time on the digital alarm clock; *it's 3:35 am.* He looks back up at the ceiling and takes a deep breath to relax. He tries to listen carefully to the distant sounds but he can't figure out. Curiosity getting the better of him, he decides to get out of bed to investigate. He grabs his dressing gown from off the back of the door and puts it on. As he makes his way slowly along the landing to the stairs, the voices seem to be getting louder. He creeps downstairs, unsure about what is he going to find. Once in the front room, he discovers the TV on and the volume down low, the kids cosied up on the couch, watching a home movie from their mom's birthday party from a few years ago. The kids notice their dad as he makes his way over to them. "Room for another?" he asks. Luke shuffles over and he sits between them. Matt's attention is drawn to the TV. Anne is speaking up close to the camera. Looking beautiful and radiant with music playing in the background, gradually, everyone falls back to sleep cuddling into each other.

Later that morning, Matt drops the kids off at his parents. Exchanging pleasantries over a cup of tea, he reels off all the errands he must work through.

Setting off to start the errands, he is driving along a busy road, listening to the radio. Matt turns left onto a slip road to join a duel carriageway. He no sooner joins the road when Anna's favourite Struts' song begins playing on the radio. Flooded with memories and thoughts, his eyes well up and he doesn't notice his speed creep up. He glances down to check; the speedometer reads nearly ninety. Applying the brakes, he checks the rear-view mirror hoping it's clear. Blue lights strobe brightly like fireworks in the mirror and are gaining rapidly. The police car manoeuvres in behind Matt. Taking the next exit, he pulls over and adjusts the volume on the radio. The police officer approaches the car and taps the driver's window with his index finger knuckle. Matt winds down the window a third of the way. "Do you know why you've been stopped?" asks the young officer in a smug way.

"I'm not sure?" replies Matt, not in the mood for any questions. With both his hands moving in a twisting action on the steering wheel, looking straight ahead.

"Speeding! You were going almost 90 MPH!" says the officer. "The speed is bad enough on that busy and dangerous stretch of road and there have already been thirty-eight deaths. That's thirty-eight families told their loved ones not coming home. How would you feel to be told you've lost a loved one?" the officer continues. Matt sits silently for a few seconds, still staring ahead. His eyes start welling up. "Did you hear me sir?" asks the officer.

"How would I feel?" replies Matt, overcome with emotions, and feels the anger and rage building. "How would I feel?" repeats Matt. He locks the door, starts the engine, selects first gear and puts his hand on the handbrake.

Realising something's not right, the officer shouts, "Excuse me, sir." Matt turns and looks up at the officer. A tear falls down his cheek.

"Let me show you!" states Matt. Sharply accelerating, the front wheels spin and give out a little smoke. The officer quickly gets back into the police car and pursues Matt. Driving like a man possessed, Matt starts to weave in and out of the traffic, taking unnecessary and dangerous risks. The police follow close behind with flashing blue lights and two-tone sirens wailing.

The police communicate with control, "In pursuit of a speeding vehicle and more assistance required." Matt continues to drive dangerously, narrowly missing head on collisions, going through red lights, and skidding around corners and roundabouts. Not thinking clearly, and full of anger and rage, he continues to drive erratically, naively thinking he's proving something. He makes his way through some streets which lead to an industrial estate, with the police car close behind. The police communicate with control and other police vehicles to help bring it to a stop. Driving through the industrial estate lined with high brick walls, Matt glances to the side road on the left, trying to decide which way to go, when a large four by four police car, seemingly out of nowhere, gives a tactical nudge to the rear wheels of Matt's car. The car is thrown into a one-hundred-and-eighty-degree spin bringing it to a dramatic halt. The police all converge on Matt's car. Smashing the window and dragging him out, Matt is placed under arrest for multiple offences.

Matt is taken to the police station where he is breathalysed, processed and put in a cell. He asks for a phone call. "Helen, it's me. I'm sorry to call you like this but I need your help. I'm in the police station," says Matt. "I've been arrested for dangerous driving. Can you get me a solicitor? Please, I didn't know who else to call," he continues.

"I'll see what I can do!" replies Helen.

Chapter 20

Matt, with a million thoughts running through his mind, can't sit still; one minute on his feet pacing around, the next minute sitting and holding his head in his hands. A few hours that feel like a few days, pass by.

The metal viewing shutter is suddenly opened by a policeman.

He closes it again and opens the cell door. Matt looks up. "Come on, you're free to go," says the policeman. In a bit of shock and disbelief, Matt makes his way out of the cell to the charging desk. The sergeant hands over his belongings. "We are giving you an official caution, sign here please." Matt, unsure of what's going on, doesn't bother asking any questions and signs. He quickly gets his things together and is shown out of the station. Once through the last set of gates, the policeman says, "Mind how you go and try to stay out of trouble." Walking along the street lined with cars, Matt hears a horn: beep, beep. Helen is sitting in her car, waiting for him.

"Jump in I'll drop you off," says Helen.

Getting in the passenger seat, Matt says, "What happened to the solicitor? Did you get me released?"

"I contacted my father who plays golf with the chief superintendent and he told him about the situation. He said he would make a few phone calls. The chief said that due to the situation and circumstances, they'll overlook the matter because you have two children and a job."

A few days go by. Matt is back at work and is about to finish for the day when Helen approaches him and asks, "Do you want a lift home? I noticed you got a taxi this morning. I've got an errand to do and I'm going past yours."

"Yeah, please, that'll be great; the car wouldn't start this morning. I was just about to phone for another taxi," Matt replies. Helen's car pulls up outside Matt's place. "So when are you able to go to the other branch next, Matt?" asks Helen, putting her hand on his leg.

"I always thought that was a terrible code word for the hotel," says Matt turning to look at Helen with a grin on his face. Looking at each other, he looks down at Helens chest and asks, "Where's the gold locket I got you?"

"I've put it down somewhere, but I can't find it. I think it'll be at home in my bedside drawer, I couldn't find it this morning," Helen replies with a sorrowful look on her face. Gazing for a moment in each other's eyes, they both look at the other's lips, they slowly lean forward and passionately kiss, touching each other's face with a hand. "Are you coming in or do you really have an errand to run?" asks Matt with a cheeky grin.

"Yes, I'm coming in, that was just for the people at work. I don't want to get a reputation for myself, do I?" she replies.

"Good, because we have the place to ourselves. Her parents have the kids for the night," states Matt.

Having had something to eat, Matt and Helen get cosy on the couch, watching TV, when Helen says, "I still can't believe Anna didn't know about us, especially after the time the she was here as I left. And you managed to keep it a secret for all this time. How long has it been, a year and a half—two years?"

"Okay, don't go on. I don't know. Yeah, about that long," replies Matt.

"Okay," says Helen with a grin, knowing she is winding him up. "Well, at least put something good on the TV," she adds.

"Where's the remote?" Matt asks. They start routing around with their hands for the remote. Matt slides off the couch onto his knees and puts his hands down the back of the cushions in search it. Helen, thinking he looks silly, smiles as she watches him fumble around. His hand sweeps to the end of the back and down the side, and comes across a bit of paper. Thinking it's strange, he pulls it out. It's an envelope with his name on. Matt sits back on the couch, perched on the edge. Looking at the envelope, it reads 'To Matt' in Anna's handwriting. Matt gets a lump in his throat and his hands start to tremble. Slowly opening the envelope, his hands shake. He discovers a letter and a familiar gold locket with five diamonds on it. He takes out the locket, opens it and holds it in the palm of his hand. He stares at a picture of him cuddling Helen: the tears heavily well up in his eyes. He takes out the letter, unfolds it and it reads, 'my dearest Matt, I hope you and Helen are very happy together, all my love, Anna x.'

Staring at the letter, a tear rolls down his cheek. He gently throws the locket towards Helen and says, "I've found the locket."